Max and the Map

Homer's Odyssey for Children

EDWARD ALAN KURTZ

CONTENTS

CHAPTER 1

The Map

Once there was a boy named Max. Max did not like having to go to school. All he wanted to do was to play games all day. He especially did not like having to go to the library at school. Books? Yuk! But sometimes he had to look for books for reports that were due.

One day Max found an old book that had been pushed back behind all the other books on the shelf. This book must have been forgotten, thought Max. It was dusty and had a dark brown leather cover. He opened the book and started to flip through the pages.

It was an old book of maps. There were maps of the oceans, and maps of the world, and maps of each of the seven continents: Europe, Asia, Africa, Australia, North America, South America, and Antarctica, although there wasn't much on that map except an awful lot of white!

Since he had to do a book report, Max thought this book of maps might be interesting. He took it up to the front desk.

"Oh, dear," said the librarian. "I've never seen this book before. Where did you find it?"

"It was sort of hidden, because it had been pushed back behind some other books," answered Max.

"Well, it looks quite interesting," said the librarian, stamping the book. "It will be due in two week."

Two weeks, thought Max. That's plenty of time. I just need to get home and get started. The sooner I finish it, the sooner I can get back to playing games. They're much more exciting than dusty old books!

Little did Max know what was soon going to happen to him because of this "dusty old book!"

He threw the book into his backpack and jumped on his bike. On the way home, he saw a group of his friends walking together down the street.

"Hey!" he yelled.

"Hi Max," said some of his friends.

"Do you want to go down to the lake with us?" asked one of his friends.

They lived near Cayuga Lake, in Ithaca, New York. They often went sailing with their families on the lake.

"No, I can't," replied Max. "I have to go home and do this stupid book report."

"What's your book report going to be about?" asked Kathy, another friend.

"It's going to be about this old book of maps I found in the library," answered Max.

"Let's see," said another friend, Brad.

Max pulled it out of his backpack and showed the dusty old book to Brad and Kathy. The other kids had already started to walk towards the lake.

"Wow," said Brad. "I never saw anything like this before. Let's have a look inside."

"Yes, let's," said Kathy.

So Max parked his bike. He and Kathy and Brad sat on the grass under a tree. Max, with the book on his lap, sat between his two best friends, Brad on his right and Kathy on his left.

The three of them looked at the old maps as Max flipped through the book. There were even maps with drawings of ancient monsters and sea creatures. They looked at the maps of the seven continents, and then the maps of the five oceans of the world: the Antarctic Ocean, the Arctic Ocean, the Atlantic Ocean, the Indian Ocean, and the Pacific Ocean.

Then they found a section that showed the many seas of the world, like the Baltic Sea, the Caribbean Sea, and the Dead Sea.

"Look at this one," said Kathy. She was pointing at a map of the Mediterranean Sea. "Here's Greece. And look at all these creatures. Some of these are very strange. What is that one?"

It looked like a giant monster, but it only had one eye.

They were all touching the same map at the same time. Suddenly things started to spin around and there was mist and darkness surrounding the three friends.

"What's happening?" asked Brad.

They were all holding onto the book now as they were spinning around. The mist got thicker and thicker. Soon they were in total darkness. And now they heard the sound of the sea.

When the mists began to clear, the three of them were sitting on the deck of a sailboat in the middle of the Mediterranean Sea!

CHAPTER 2

The Storm

The three friends sat in silence for a while. They were in shock. They had no idea what was going on, or where they were.

"What happened?" cried Kathy.

"Where are we?" shouted Brad.

Just my luck, thought Max. I find a book in the library and end up in some weird dream!

"We're not on Cayuga Lake, that's for sure," said Max.

"How can you tell?" asked Kathy.

"Smell the air," answered Max.

Brad and Kathy both tilted their heads up a little and smelled the air.

"What do you smell?" asked Brad.

"Salt," answered Max.

Kathy and Brad sniffed again.

"You're right," said Kathy. "It is salty air. We must be in an ocean."

"Or a sea," said Brad. "Remember the last thing we were looking at was a map of the Mediterranean Sea."

"That's right," said Max.

"Do you two actually think we are somewhere in the middle of the Mediterranean Sea?" asked Kathy.

"Can't tell at the moment," answered Max. "But at least we all know how to sail a boat."

They lived near Cayuga Lake and had learned how to sail long before they had even started to go to school. Sailing was what they did every weekend with their families. And now that they were a little older, sometimes they were allowed to sail on their own. But not in stormy weather.

So that was the good news: they all knew how to sail, and they were all pretty good at it. The bad news was the weather. Although it was sunrise and starting to get light, they could see a huge dark black cloud coming towards them.

"And any good sailor knows what we have to do when we see that," said Max as he pointed towards the massive cloud. "Let's start taking down these sails. And put on your life preservers."

He put his backpack around his chest before he put on his life preserver. The three of them worked as quickly as they could. They had just finished when the storm hit their boat. The rain was coming down in buckets, and the wind nearly blew them overboard. But they all held on.

"Here we go!" shouted Max above the noise of the wind.

In addition to the terrible wind and the pounding rain, the waves were becoming quite violent. The little sailboat was being tossed around like it was just a tiny piece of cork in the middle of the ocean.

All three of them were using cups and whatever they could find to scoop up water from the deck and throw it into the sea. Part of this water was from the pouring rain, but most of it was from the incredible waves that poured over the sides of the boat.

The pitching of the waves threw them down onto the deck from time to time. They would have complained about all this – the wind and the rain and being thrown to the deck of the boat – but they were too busy just trying to keep from being tossed overboard.

"Look out!" cried Kathy.

Brad and Max looked to where Kathy was pointing. A massive wave, the size of a building, was just about to sweep over them.

There was a deafening crash and then everything went black.

CHAPTER 3

The Island

Max felt very wet, but very warm. He had a nasty fishy taste in his mouth. He slowly opened his eyes and squinted because of the bright sun. He was on a sandy beach and is must have been about noon, judging by the position of the sun.

He pushed himself up from the sand and looked around. Things were starting to come back to him: the book, the map, the boat, the storm, his friends.

His friends! Where were they? Were they okay? He yelled out, "Kathy! Brad!" He looked far to the left down the sandy beach and saw something. He ran. It was Kathy.

He lifted her up and tried to shake her. She promptly spit a mouthful of salt water into his face.

"Geez, thanks," said Max.

She was coming to. Her eyes slowly opened.

"Max?" she asked.

"Yes," he answered. "Are you okay?"

"Yes, I think so," she answered. "What happened? Where are we?"

"The storm must have wrecked us here on this beach," he answered. "But I have no idea yet where we are. We must find Brad."

He helped her stand up and then they both started to shout for Brad and look for him. They decided to split up: Kathy went farther to the left and Max went to the right, passing the place where he had been washed ashore.

They eventually met back in the middle of the beach. Kathy had walked as far as she could to the left, and then she had come to a cliff. There was no more beach. Max had walked as far as he could to the right, and he had also come to a cliff. So they were on a cove and there was no sign of Brad.

"What are we going to do about Brad?" asked Kathy.

"Let's walk inland a little bit," answered Max. "I saw a path about halfway along the beach."

They came to the path and they suddenly had a little hope: there were footprints in the sand leading into the path.

"Brad!" cried Kathy.

"Maybe," said Max. "We'll just have to follow the path and the footsteps and find out."

They walked away from the sea. They were both tired and hungry, but mostly thirsty. They soon came to a open area where there were some huts. There were people here, but they all seemed to be asleep under some shade trees.

It was just then that Kathy gave a little cry: it was Brad. He too was sleeping under a tree, next to a group of these strangers.

She and Max tried to shake Brad awake. He opened his eyes just a little. He didn't seem all that happy to see Max and Kathy. It seemed like he was more interested in sleeping.

Max shook him hard. "Brad," said Max. "What has happened to you?

"These nice people gave me some of that sweet juice over there," answered Brad. "And now, if you don't mind, I'd like to take a nap." And with that, he fell back to sleep again.

Max and Kathy walked over to the large clay jug. They both smelled it. It smelled pleasant enough, but they were both smart enough not to drink it. They did find water to drink and some fruit, so at least they had enough energy so that they could continue on their adventure.

They walked back over to Brad and shook him awake again. He was a little bit more awake this time, and definitely grouchy.

"I want more juice," he said.

"No way," said Max. "We have to find a way out of here."

"But why," said Brad. "I like it here."

"We have to get home to Ithaca," said Kathy.

"First we have to find out if our little sailboat is still around," said Max.

"It's over there," said Brad, as he groggily pointed over towards another beach.

It took plenty of convincing, but they finally talked Brad into going back to the boat. And just in time: the sleepy people were starting to wake up. The three

venturers ran, jumped into the boat, and were far out into the sea by the time the sleep-walkers staggered onto the beach.

"Where do we go now?" asked Kathy.

CHAPTER 4

The Monster

The sailboat had not been damaged. This was quite a miracle. It had blown right up onto the protected sandy cove where the three had just run to escape the oversleeping strangers.

As they moved farther away from the island, they realized that it was not very large. And just a bit to the right was a larger area of land. Whether it was another island or the mainland, they weren't able to tell. But they hoisted the sails and made their way towards it, because they were hungry and needed to find some more water.

"And no more juice," said Max.

Brad smiled.

Soon they were nearing the land. They found a beach and they left the sailboat there. Again, they found a path that lead away from the beach and into the interior of the land.

"Maybe we'll find something to eat and some water here," said Max.

Brad and Kathy followed him as they walked on the path. Soon they came to large hill. The path led around it and past a large opening. It was a cave.

"I guess we should check inside," said Max. "It's hard to tell what we'll find in there."

They went into the cave. It was not as dark as they had thought, because the opening was quite large and it allowed a good bit of sunlight in.

It was someone's home! There was a table and chairs and a bed. There was also food! There was food, plenty of food, right there on the table! They knew it wasn't right to steal, but they were starving, so they helped themselves.

As they were eating, Max said, "Have you noticed anything strange about this room?"

"What do you mean?" asked Kathy between bites.

"Everything is so big," answered Max. "The chairs are big, the table is big, and look at the size of that bed."

Just then they heard an eardrum-breaking roar. It was

a giant man! No wonder all the furniture was so big. And he was wearing a patch over one of his eyes, just like the picture that Kathy had seen on the map!

The three of them were scared to death. They backed away from the table and stood in a corner of the cave. The giant man laughed and turned to walk away. How strange, they thought.

But in the next few seconds they understood why he had laughed. He pushed an enormous boulder in front of the entrance to the cave and they were plunged into darkness.

"Now what?" asked Brad.

"I don't know," answered Max. "I guess we have to sit tight and see what happens. I don't see any way out of this, at least not now."

"And there is no other way out of the cave, right?" asked Kathy.

"Not that I saw," answered Max.

"Me neither," said Brad.

"Since we've eaten and since it's dark, we might as well get some rest," said Max. "I'm sure we'll wake up when he comes back."

"Yeah," said Kathy. "He's not exactly the quiet type."

They found the floor of the cave very uncomfortable for a nap.

"Well," said Max. "We've already made ourselves at home by eating his food: we might as well try his bed."

As it was a huge bed, there was plenty of room for the three of them. They got some much needed rest. Later they were awakened by the sound of the giant man slowly moving the boulder away from the entrance to the cave.

They quickly got off the giant man's bed. Max grabbed his backpack and threw it to Brad. Then he motioned for Brad and Kathy to stand on either side of the entrance to the cave. He grabbed one of the mugs off of the table and filled it with sand from the floor of the cave.

The giant man had finally pushed the boulder the whole way to the side of the entrance to the cave. Just as he entered, Max jumped out from the shadows and threw the sand into the man's eye.

Run!" he yelled.

Caught by surprise, the big slow giant man tried to get the sand out of his eye and didn't see that his captors were escaping. They ran the whole way back to the sailboat and were just a stone's throw from shore when the giant man arrived on the beach, yelling and waving his arms.

"That was a close call," said Kathy. "What's next?"

Aeolus the God of Wind.

CHAPTER 5

The Winds

After narrowly escaping the clutches of the one-eyed man, they sailed away from that island. Again, the farther away from the island they sailed, they could see that it wasn't a very big island.

"You know," said Kathy. "When all of this started, we were looking at a map of the Mediterranean Sea. Right?"

"Right," responded Max and Brad.

"And do you remember that on that map we saw a picture of a monster with one eye?" she asked.

"Yes," they said.

"So I think we are somewhere in the Mediterranean Sea," she said.

"You're probably right," said Max.

"And it seems like there are lots of tiny islands," said Kathy.

"We might be able to figure out where we are if we look at that map again," said Brad.

"Let's get it out and have a look," said Max.

There wasn't much wind at the moment, so they were slowly sailing towards yet another small island.

They sat down, just like they had been sitting under the shade tree back in Ithaca, and looked for the map with the one-eyed monster on it.

"There," said Kathy. "See it: there's the one-eyed monster. It's on a very tiny island in the Mediterranean Sea."

"Yes," said Max. "And there's another small island just next to it. I think that's the island where we almost lost Brad."

Brad grinned. "If you guys had only tasted it, you would know why I drank so much of it."

"You do too much of anything, and it's not going to be good for you," said Kathy.

"Now you're starting to sound like my mom!" joked Brad.

They were always teasing each other, almost like

brother and sister.

Meanwhile, Max was looking closely at the map.

"There's one more island near this last one," he said. "Since the wind has died down, maybe the tide will take us over there."

Now they could see the island. It wasn't that far away, and, yes, the tide was taking them in that direction.

Eventually they entered a small bay. There was a man standing on the beach waving for them to come towards him. After they pulled the sailboat up onto the beach, they walked over to him.

He didn't speak English, of course, but he made gestures to show that he had food for them, if they would follow him.

They walked away from the beach down a path to a small hut not far away. The man gave them some food and some water. They were all tired again, so Kathy and Brad sat up against the wall on the outside of the hut and took a nap.

In the meantime, the man was trying to explain something to Max. He kept blowing air out of his mouth, and finally Max figured out it had something to do with the wind. He also gave Max a leather bag, and again it had something to do with the wind.

He motioned towards the beach and the sailboat, so Max woke up Kathy and Brad. The four of them walked down to the beach and the man motioned for them to get into the boat. They pushed off and waited to see what this was all about.

There had been absolutely no breeze for quite some time now. Suddenly, as the man stood on the beach and blew air out of his mouth, the most amazing thing happened: a huge wind picked up and blew the sailboat very swiftly out of the bay! They barely had a chance to wave goodbye to the man on the beach.

Since Max had not taken a nap, he decided to get a little rest. As he was sleeping, Brad and Kathy noticed the leather bag the man had given Max. Brad was very curious: he wanted to open the bag.

"Don't do that!" yelled Kathy.

But it was too late. It was a bag of wind that was supposed to help them in the future if there was no wind. But Brad had opened it at the wrong time and in a few minutes they were back on the same beach. The man was still standing there. They were back where they had started.

"Any more bright ideas?" Kathy asked Brad.

CHAPTER 6

The Giants

By this time Max was awake: the wind that blew them back to the man on the beach was very loud, just like a hurricane.

The man didn't seem to have another bag of wind to give them, but at least he got them started again. They turned around and he blew them out of the bay and back into the sea. This time there was enough wind out at sea to get them to the next island.

They looked at the map again while they were sailing.

"It's another small island in this chain of islands," said Max.

"There are no pictures, so it's hard to tell what we'll find there," said Kathy.

"Hopefully no more one-eyed giants," said Brad.

"Hopefully no more juice," Kathy teased.

They sailed towards a bay on this island. As they

were coming around a cliff on entering the bay, a huge rock came plummeting down into the water. It narrowly missed hitting the little sailboat. They all looked up but didn't see anything.

"Must have been an accident," said Brad.

"I'm not sure," said Max. He had a sixth sense and was aware of possible dangers.

They landed on the tiny beach in the bay. Again, they were looking for food, water, shelter, help, anything to help them get back to Ithaca. They left the sailboat and walked around the beach until they found a path.

They followed the path inland. They could see some smoke coming up from the ground off in the distance. They eventually came to the edge of a clearing and were amazed at the size of the huts around the smoking fire: more giants!

They had just decided that this was not a safe place to be looking for anything, when they heard a loud voice thundering behind them. Actually, it was more or less thundering above them, because it was, in fact, a giant. A two-eyed giant. And it had a certain hungry look in its eye, or, rather, eyes.

"Run!" shouted Max.

But the giant had already grabbed Kathy. It had dropped its spear, so, thinking fast, Max picked up the spear. It was big, but Max was able to handle it. He rammed it down onto the top of the giant's foot.

The giant dropped Kathy. Brad caught Kathy. The giant was hopping up and down on one foot. Max and Brad and Kathy were already running towards the beach and the sailboat. The giant picked up his spear and threw it with all his might at the three fleeing friends, but he missed them by a mile. He obviously wasn't one of the better spear-throwers on the island.

They reached the sailboat and pushed it out into the bay. Kathy and Brad started to paddle while Max put up the sails. They thought they were safe, but just as they were going past the same cliff on their way out of the bay, another huge rock crashed down into the water right next to the sailboat. The good news was that it actually propelled them farther away from the bay. The bad news was that there were more rocks to come.

They looked up and, standing on the cliff, were dozens of giants. They had heard the commotion back at their huts when Max had speared the giant's foot. Now they had all come out in force to seek revenge. Boulder after boulder rocked the little sailboat. But, fortunately for Max and his friends, the giants were as bad at throwing rocks as they were at throwing spears.

"I don't know about you two," said Max. "But I sure am tired of dealing with giants!"

"Me too," said Kathy.

"Ditto," said Brad.

CHAPTER 7

The Witch

They were back at sea again, sailing away from the giants' island, and looking at the map and trying to figure out what they should do next.

"I think that this is the giants' island," said Kathy, pointing to a tiny spot in the middle of the Mediterranean Sea.

"Yes," said Max. "You're right. And it looks like there's yet another tiny island to the east of that one."

They all looked out across the sea. It was a little hazy, but off in the distance, there was, in fact, the small island that they could see on the map.

"Oh, I hope there are no giants on this island," said Brad.

"Me too," said Max. "And we really need to get something to eat and some water to drink. I'm starving!'

"Me too," said Kathy.

They were able to find a small beach where they easily dragged the sailboat up onto the sand. Looking over towards a hill, they saw a women standing. She was motioning for them to come with her.

"I don't know," said Max. "I don't have a good feeling about this."

"But we have to eat," said Kathy. "Maybe she'll give us some food and water."

"At least she's not a giant," said Brad.

"Okay," said Max. "Let's go."

When the woman saw that the three visitors were coming towards her, she turned and started to walk down the other side of the hill, away from the beach. The three followed her and soon they arrived at a hut that was surrounded by gardens and pens with livestock, like pigs and goats.

The woman was waiting for them at the door and she invited them inside. There they found a scrumptious meal: they couldn't resist. When you've gone without food, and you know what true hunger feels like, everything you put in your mouth tastes so wonderful!

The woman offered them something to drink, but it was in a large clay jug, and Max's sixth sense told him not to try it. Brad was more than willing to taste it, after his experience with the juice he had enjoyed on the other island. Kathy was so thirsty she didn't care what happened: she was going to drink something.

The woman became very insistent that Max try the liquid from the jug. He allowed her to put some in a clay cup, and then pretended to drink some of it. It was a good thing that he didn't because suddenly, right before his eyes, there were two pigs sitting at the table where Brad and Kathy had been sitting.

This woman was a witch and she had changed them into pigs! Brad's table manners left something to be desired, and his mother had often told him he was as messy as a pig. But this was different: they were actually pigs grunting and looking around on the floor for something to eat!

She patiently waited for Max to turn into a pig, but he had outsmarted her. She didn't know that he had only pretended to drink from the cup. He turned the cup upside-down and poured the contents out onto the floor.

The witch was smiling: she was quite amazed that this young boy had outsmarted her. She opened an old chest and pulled out another clay jug. She poured this liquid into a bowl and placed it in front of the two pigs. They began to drink it and soon there was a boy and a girl down on the floor on their hands and knees lapping up something out of a bowl.

Max was laughing hysterically! "Look at you two," he said.

Kathy and Brad looked at each other and then up at Max and the witch, and then all four of them started to laugh.

"What happened?" asked Kathy, as she and Brad got up off of the floor.

"Whatever you drank from the clay jug turned you into pigs," said Max.

"Why didn't you turn into a pig," asked Brad.

"I didn't drink any: I just pretended to," answered Max.

After this the witch gave them more food to take with them, and some water: real water! They thanked her and, as they got into their sailboat, she pointed in the direction she thought was best for them to try. Then she got down on her hands and knees and started making grunting noises. She started laughing so hard that she fell over onto the sand.

"What a clown!" said Max.

CHAPTER 8

The Wizard

As they got underway, Max pulled the map out from his backpack. He wanted to have an idea of where it was that the witch was sending them.

It looked like she was sending them to a larger island farther away from the string of smaller island they had visited so far. On the map it also appeared as a black island, unlike the other islands that were drawn to look like the color of sand or earth.

"What do you think?" asked Kathy.

"I'm not sure," answered Max. "I think that she wasn't a bad witch, really. I think she was just having a bit of fun. So I can't see that she would be sending us into a dangerous situation."

"I agree," said Brad.

In the distance they saw the land stretching far to the left and to the right. It was, for sure, a much larger island than the others. And, indeed, it did look black:

there was a huge dark cloud that seemed to hover permanently over the entire island, even though it was a clear sky otherwise.

They found a bay and pulled the sailboat up onto the beach.

"I wonder what we're going to find this time," said Brad.

They were soon welcomed by several people who seemed friendly enough. They motioned the three travelers to follow them along a path that led through a small grove of trees.

"Did you see that?" asked Max.

"What?" asked the other two.

"That guy just walked through a tree," answered Max.

"You're kidding," said Kathy.

"No, he's not," said Brad. "I just saw another guy walk through a tree."

"This is spooky," said Kathy.

"This is more than spooky," said Max. "I think they're ghosts, and we might be in for some serious trouble.

Let's just play it cool for now, and see what happens."

The ghosts led them to a cave, and they all went inside. This cave was not nearly as light as the one-eyed giant man's cave. It was because the entrance was much smaller. Once their eyes had adjusted they were able to see better.

The room was full of ghosts, men and women, some standing, some walking, and some sitting around talking with each other. In a way it was spooky, and in another way it wasn't quite as scary as they thought it might have been.

An old ghost with long white hair and a long white beard came towards them. They were a little afraid, but he seemed to be a gentle kind of a ghost.

"Welcome to our island," said the ghost.

"You speak English!" they all said at the same time.

"Yes," said the ghost. "I am a wizard, and I already know who you are, where you come from, and what you seek."

"Wow!" said the three friends.

"You are Max, Kathy and Brad, and you come from

Ithaca," said the wizard.

"Cool!" said the three friends.

"What are we seeking?" asked Max.

"You are seeking a way to return home to Ithaca," answered the wizard.

"Awesome," said Brad.

"Will we find our way home?" asked Kathy.

"You still have many adventures that await you," answered the wizard.

"But will we get back to Ithaca?" asked Max.

"The path ahead will be difficult and you will meet many challenges," replied the wizard.

"Adventures and difficulties and challenges, yeah, yeah, yeah," said Brad impatiently. "But are we going to get home or aren't we!"

"Your journey home will be full of new experiences," answered the wizard.

"Well, at least he mentioned the word 'home' this time," said Kathy.

"But you must first return to the island of the witch," said the wizard.

The three looked at each other.

"Why do we have to go back to see her?" asked Max. "She turned my two friends here into pigs."

The wizard started howling with laughter. "Did she, now?" he asked.

"Yes," said Max. "And it was embarrassing. I didn't drink anything from the jug that she offered, so I didn't turn into a pig."

"We were on the ground drinking from a big bowl when we turned back into humans," said Brad.

"And you both were grunting, don't forget," added Max.

"Thanks for reminding us," said Kathy.

"In any event, back to the witch you must go," continued the wizard. "She will give you information about the rest of your journey."

"She talks?" asked Brad.

"Yes," answered the wizard.

"English?" asked Max.

"Yes," answered the wizard.

"Thank heavens for that," said Kathy.

CHAPTER 9

Return to the Witch

The three said goodbye to the wizard and returned to the beach. They got into their sailboat and sailed back the way they had come, back to the witch's island. They looked behind as they left, and the island was black as ever, with the big dark cloud hanging over it.

The farther away they got from the black island, the brighter and clearer the sky got. They could see the witch's island in the distance and soon they were sailing up to the beach where they had recently left.

The amazing thing was the witch was there, just as before, as if she had never left. She was just standing there, waiting for them to arrive.

"Hello again," said Max.

"Welcome again," said the witch.

"Why didn't you tell us you could speak English?" asked Kathy.

"You didn't ask me," replied the witch with a toothless grin.

"The wizard from the black island over there said we were supposed to come back here, that you would tell us things we need to know about the rest of our trip," said Max.

"Yes," said the witch. "Please follow me. We can have another meal together."

"Just watch what you serve us," said Brad.

The witch giggled. "I was just having a bit of fun, you know," she said.

Back at her hut, she put some fruit and water on the table and invited the three of them to sit down with her. She put a candle in the center of the table and closed the door of the hut. It was quite dark inside the hut, with just a small amount of light coming from the candle.

"I must ask for complete silence!" she said dramatically.

Their eyes got big. They thought she was listening for some kind of voice to help her explain to them what the future was going to hold. They waited in anticipation. The only thing they could hear was their own breathing.

"Oh, it's okay," she said. "I thought that goat in the pen was asking for something."

The three visitors looked at each other, not knowing what she was up to.

Then she giggled hysterically.

"Let us begin!" she said very seriously. She began to chant a spell:

"Eye of newt

And tooth of hen,

Give us facts

Of where and when!"

"Hens don't have teeth," Kathy whispered to the other two.

"Silence!" shouted the witch. But then she started giggling again. Soon she was serious:

"Eye of newt

And tooth of...

Tooth of...

Tooth of..."

She was stuck!

"Rabbit?" said Kathy.

"How am I ever going to come up with something that rhymes with rabbit?" asked the witch.

"Habit?" said Kathy.

"Do you really know what you're doing?" asked Brad.

"Do you want to get home or do you want to become a pig again?" asked the witch.

Brad shut his mouth.

"Try cow," suggested Max. "There are lots of things that rhyme with cow."

"Okay," said the witch. She started again:

"Eye of newt

And tooth of cow,

Show us the future

And do it right now!"

The three visitors couldn't help but laugh.

"That was terrible," said Kathy.

"Can't you come up with something better than that?" asked Brad.

"Don't make me get that jug out again!" said the witch.

"Maybe you can just explain what we need to know without all the chanting stuff," said Max.

"Oh, all right," said the witch. "You take all the fun out of it."

She sighed. "Here goes," she said. "First, beware of the singing mermaids."

"Singing mermaids?" asked Brad.

"Do I hear an echo in here?" said the witch. "Second, beware of monsters: two monsters, one of which is a whirlpool and the other one has six heads."

"You're making this up!" said Kathy.

"I am not," said the witch. "Look: do you want help or not?"

"Yes," said Max. "Please go ahead."

"Okay, right," said the witch. "Now where was I? Oh, yes, let's see: mermaids, monsters, oh, yes: be careful not to eat anything you find on your own on any of these islands. Just wait until someone offers you something."

"Is that it?" asked Brad.

"Pretty much so," answered the witch.

"And we are going to get home, right?" asked Max.

"Eye of newt, Tooth of..." started the witch.

"Oh, please," said Kathy. "Do we have to go through that again?"

"Yes," said the witch. "I have to start back at the beginning if I'm going to remember it all."

"Can you just tell us if we'll make it back to Ithaca safely?" asked Max.

"I see an island," said the witch. "I see many islands, as a matter of fact; and a shipwreck; and friendly people helping you; and a lake in a far off land."

"That'll be Cayuga Lake!" said Kathy.

"All right!" said Brad.

CHAPTER 10

The Singing Mermaids

Before they left her island, the witch explained to the three voyagers what they would need to do if they came across the singing mermaids. The songs that the mermaids sang were dangerous. She gave them some wax and told them to use it to plug their ears.

It wasn't very clear to them how a song could be so dangerous, but they accepted the wax and got their sailboat ready for the next part of their adventure.

After they left the witch's island, they traveled in a different direction than that of the black island. They headed to the east of the black island and soon saw what looked like a very beautiful island. Even at a great distance they could tell that it was much green-er than any of the other islands they had visited so far. All the other islands were quite dry and dusty.

As they got closer they could see that the land was covered in lush forests. They could even see a beautiful waterfall in the interior of the island.

"We've got to stop here," said Brad.

"Yes," said Kathy. "Everything is so green and lush. There's bound to be fresh water and food here."

"I'm not sure," said Max. "Things aren't always what they appear to be. Besides, I can't see a place to land here. There's no beach: only rocks."

"You're right," said Kathy. "Maybe we'll have to sail around it to find a beach."

"It doesn't look like it's a very big island," added Brad.

They began to sail around the island, first to the left, then around to the opposite side of the island, and then back around the right side to where they had started.

"I don't want to give up the chance of finding food and water," said Max. "But I also don't want to risk damaging the sailboat on the rocks."

It was just about then that they saw something swimming down below them. The water was perfectly clear, so they knew right away what it was: it was their first mermaid!

"Quick," said Max. "Take some of this wax."

He gave a little to both Brad and Kathy.

"Hurry," he said. "Roll it up into two balls of wax and stuff one into each of your ears."

Brad and Kathy had just finished putting the wax in their ears when there was a bump under the sailboat. One of the mermaids had banged into the boat with enough force to knock Max over. He fell onto the deck and the rest of the wax fell into the sea.

By now, the mermaids were sitting on the rocks near the sailboat. They were quite lovely and they began to sing their magical song.

Max began to smile. He began to steer the sailboat towards the mermaids, towards the rocks. Brad and Kathy couldn't believe what he was doing! He was going to crash the sailboat into the rocks!

Brad tried to steer the boat away from the rocks, but Max pushed him away. Kathy and Brad signaled to each other and they wrestled Max to the deck of the sailboat. Brad sat on top of him while Kathy quickly steered away from the rocks, just in the nick of time.

When the mermaids saw that the boat was moving away from the rocks, they jumped into the water and started swimming towards the sailboat. They were incredibly fast swimmers and it was only because there was a strong wind, and because Kathy was a good sailor that they were able to escape the mermaids.

"It was just so beautiful," said Max later on, when they were away from the island. "I just wanted to be on the island: I didn't care about the rocks or the boat or anything else."

"It's a good thing we were able to wrestle you to the deck," said Brad.

"And that Brad was able to keep you there while I steered," said Kathy. "We were just inches away from losing our boat."

Max was still hearing the voices of the singing mermaids in his mind. "So beautiful," he said.

"Snap out of it!" said Kathy.

CHAPTER 11

Two Sea Monsters

After they escaped the singing mermaids, the three travelers weren't exactly sure in which direction they were supposed to go. But they needn't have worried: there was no wind to speak of. Strangely enough, the sailboat was definitely moving towards the east again. And it was moving surprisingly fast.

"There must be a very strong current in these waters," said Max.

"We're moving faster than we've ever moved with the wind in our sails," said Brad.

Then they saw it, off in the distance. They had never seen anything like it before. It was a giant whirlpool and they were headed right for it!

"Yikes!" cried Kathy. "What are we going to do?"

"There's no way out of this," said Max. "There's no wind, and even if there was, I doubt if it would be strong enough to battle this current."

"We better put on our life preservers," said Brad.

While he and Kathy put on their life preservers, Max strapped his backpack around his chest and then his life preserver on his back.

The water was churning and swirling. The little sailboat was like a tiny piece of driftwood in the strong current. They started going around in a big circle, and soon they were going faster and faster as they got closer to the center of the whirlpool.

Suddenly, just when they thought they were done for, the whirlpool spat the sailboat up out of the center. It was with such a strong force that they ended up far, far away from the whirlpool. They were out of danger for now.

"Good thing we were all holding on to the sailboat," said Max.

They were out of danger, but only temporarily.

"Remember what the witch said?" asked Kathy.

"What?" asked Brad and Max.

"Didn't she say there would be two monsters?" asked Kathy.

"That's right," said Brad.

"One down and one to go," said Max.

"I wonder if the two monsters will be back to back, or if they'll be spread out," said Kathy.

"I think we're about to find out," said Max.

"What do you mean?" asked Brad.

"Look over at that island," said Max.

After they had been spat out of the whirlpool monster, the force was still carrying them across the sea with great strength. They were approaching yet another island, whether they wanted to or not.

What Max had seen was the six-headed monster. It was sitting on top of a cliff on one side of the island, and the sailboat was heading right for it.

"Giants and ghosts and witches and warlocks are one things," said Max. "But this is getting ridiculous! Why did I ever choose this map book!"

"Well, we've made it this far," said Kathy.

"We just need to come up with a plan," added Brad.

They were getting closer to the cliff now and they could see the monster more clearly. It did, in fact, have six heads, and it was rather frightening to look at. All the heads were at the end of its long necks, and they were all bobbing about, quite excited about the approach of their next meal.

"If anyone has a plan, speak now, or we're done for," said Max.

They were just about to sail right next to the cliff, right under the six hungry mouths, when the most amazing thing happened. There was a huge rumbling noise and pieces of the cliff started to fall off. Suddenly there was an enormous explosion and the cliff and the very hungry and very confused looking six-headed monster crashed to the rocks below. This caused a tidal wave which quickly pushed the little sailboat far away from the cliffs and the very disappointed looking six-headed monster.

"Well," said Max. "I don't know whose plan that was, but it worked like a charm."

CHAPTER 12

The Orange Island

Once again, the three voyagers were pushed along without the help of the wind. The crash of the cliff along with the weight of the six-headed monster was strong enough to push them nearly as far as the next island.

"Two monsters down, and none to go," said Brad.

"Let's hope that nutty witch was right," said Kathy.

"I agree," said Max. "She was kind of kooky, but she's been right so far."

They came to the next island and found a beach. They were happy about this, because the last two islands, the Singing Mermaid Island and the Six-Headed Monster Island, had no beaches and only rocks.

They pulled the sailboat up onto the beach and looked for a path. They found one on the right side of the beach. This led up a hill and then across a wide plain. Here they found a grove of oranges.

"We should stuff your backpack full of these," said Brad.

"I don't know," said Max. "You remember what the witch said about taking food. Maybe we should walk beyond this grove and see if we can find any people to help us."

This seemed like a sensible plan, so they continued to walk. At the end of the orange grove they saw a hut. There were a couple of people working around the hut, tending their garden and their livestock.

"Are these the friendly ones the witch talked about?" asked Kathy.

"No, I think they come later," answered Max.

"Let's just hope they don't have six heads," joked Brad.

The three travelers went close to the hut to ask the people for some food. They didn't speak English, but they were willing to share their food and water.

The three sailors felt drowsy after the meal, not because of what they had eaten, but because of all the excitement and activities of the day. They followed the example of the island people and took a nap under the shade of a couple of orange trees at the edge of the grove.

When Max woke up, he saw that his backpack was missing. And so was Brad! He was afraid of what this meant: was Brad taking oranges from the grove and putting them in the backpack?

Max quietly woke up Kathy and motioned for her to join him. They tiptoed away from the sleeping islanders. When they were out of hearing distance, they decided they needed to find Brad and then be on their way.

Their first guess was a good one: there he was, picking oranges from a tree farther down a row of trees in the grove.

"Brad!" yelled Max. "Stop! We're going to get into trouble."

But it was too late. Not only had Brad filled up Max's backpack, but the islanders who had shared their meal with them, were running towards them.

"Run!" cried Kathy.

The islanders were carrying some gardening tools and they obviously weren't running on their way to do some gardening.

Max was first to reach the sailboat. He pushed it just a few feet out into the water. Kathy was next. She jumped into the boat. Brad was last, because the backpack had gotten quite heavy with all the oranges he had picked. He tossed the backpack to Max and then jumped into the boat.

The islanders were running down the hill and across the beach. They threw their heavy garden tools at the boat but they were just a little too late. The sailboat was already out of range.

Meanwhile Brad was unloading the backpack and looking at all the big round oranges.

"You almost got us killed!" cried Kathy.

"Orange you glad we got away," answered Brad.

CHAPTER 13

Prisoners

They had escaped that island and were wondering what would happen next. The wind had picked up, so they were able to use the sails to take them to the next island.

This island looked quite nice from a distance. And, as they got closer, they saw that it was almost as nice as the Singing Mermaid Island. In fact, it was even better, because it had a sandy beach. They sailed into the little protected bay and then pulled the sailboat up onto the beach.

At the back of the beach there were some shade trees. Under one of these trees sat a beautiful woman. The three adventurers slowly and cautiously went towards her.

"Do you think she might be one of the people that the witch said would help us to get back to Ithaca?" asked Brad.

"I'm not sure," said Max. "I can't remember now: did

the help come first or the shipwreck?"

"I can't remember either," said Kathy.

By now they were close to the woman. She didn't speak, but motioned for them to follow her. They were hoping that she was going to help them, so they followed her.

She led them to a hut under some shade trees away from the beach. She offered them some food and water and then, after they started eating, she left the hut. By the time they had finished eating she had returned. They just figured she had been tending her garden or vineyards or her livestock.

Although they couldn't speak her language, they tried to thank her. Then they retraced their steps back to the beach.

When they got there, they were in for a shock: their sailboat was gone!

"What a nightmare!" said Max. "What next?"

"Max, look," said Kathy. She was pointing at the woman who had followed them, and was now once again sitting under a shade tree.

"What?" answered Max.

"She's smiling," said Kathy.

"So," said Brad.

"Look at that smile," said Kathy. "That's not a normal smile. She did something with our sailboat."

They walked towards the woman who sat peacefully smiling.

"Where's our sailboat?" asked Max.

"What did you do?" asked Brad.

Of course, she didn't understand a word they were saying, but they sensed that she knew what they wanted. She just smiled, got up from her chair, and walked away, back into the trees.

"Oh great," said Kathy. "Now what do we do?"

"We could make a raft," suggested Brad.

"We could," said Max. "But sailboats don't just disappear into thin air."

"Not in our world," said Kathy. "But we're in a world of giants and monsters and witches. Anything can happen."

"Maybe," said Max. "But if she was using magic, she could have done it from her hut, right? I think she's just hidden it. Let's have a good look."

They spread out. It was easy to walk along the beach, and easy to see that there was no boat there.

"What about back in those trees?" asked Brad.

"There would be tracks in the sand," said Max. "I'm sure she she's hidden it somewhere out along the rocks or maybe under a cliff.

The rocks and cliffs were a little trickier. They searched for a really long time and were getting tired and frustrated. Just then Kathy saw something they had missed: there was a very low cave right at sea level, under a cliff that hung out over the water.

They had a hard time getting over the rocks, but they finally got to the cave. And there it was: the rope was safely tied around a rock, and the boat was part of the way up out of the water.

"Let's get out of here," said Kathy.

"I agree," said Brad. "Food or no food, she was trying to force us to stay here."

"I guess this is one case where we don't need to go back and say thank you," said Max.

They unloosened the rope, pushed the boat into the water and were out into the open sea before the strange woman knew what had happened.

CHAPTER 14

Shipwreck

As they left the island they could all see dark clouds off in the distance. But they really wanted to get away from this island, so they continued sailing, hoping that the clouds would go the other way.

Unfortunately, the sailboat acted like a magnet. The boat seemed to draw the clouds right towards it. Could it be that the woman on the beach was yet another witch? Could she control the winds and the clouds?

It didn't matter what the cause was, but the three sailors could tell that they were in for another bad storm. There was plenty of wind, and for a while they were able to keep just ahead of the storm. But soon it was pouring with rain, the wind was unbelievably strong, and the three of them prepared for the worst.

And, the worst happened.

It was so dark and rainy and windy that they could

hardly tell which way was up. The little sailboat was violently tossed around and the three of them held on for dear life.

But then it happened. The sailboat hit the rocks of yet another island, and the three brave sailors were tossed into the sea. The sailboat was no more: it was just bits and pieces crashing up against the rocks.

With strong violent waves hitting the rocks, people can get seriously hurt. So it was a miracle that in the darkness they were able to find their way up the rocks and then across the rocks above the waves.

The storm had separated them, but they were all safe. They each found a dry place and slept, knowing that there was nothing else to be done. They each knew that they had to wait until morning, until there was light. Then they could look and hopefully find each other.

The sun began to rise. The storm had ended. They came out of their dry places and started calling out for each other. Max and Kathy found each other first; and not too much later they found Brad.

They were all exhausted despite having slept, but the good news was that they were safe and no one had gotten hurt. It was sad to see bits of their faithful little sailboat along the rocks, but they had to keep going.

"Let's review," said Max. "We've done the two monsters, the island where we weren't supposed to take any food, and now the shipwreck."

"So the helpful friendly people should be next, right?" asked Brad.

"Let's hope so," said Kathy. "What's that noise?"

They heard voices and people laughing. They followed the sounds and found some young women washing clothes in a stream. The stream ran from the center of the island down until it emptied into the sea.

"Do you speak English?" asked Max.

They were very shy and were giggling a lot. Finally they gently pushed one young woman towards them. She didn't want to go, but they insisted.

"Do you speak English?" Max asked her.

"A little," she answered.

"We lost our boat in the storm last night," said Max.

"Can someone help us here?"

She explained to the others what the stranger had said. They talked a little and then she returned to Max.

"You can go talk to the king," she said.

"The king?" asked Brad.

"Yes," she answered. "The palace is over that hill. You can follow us. We're finished now."

"Thank you very much," said Kathy.

The three visitors followed the group over the hill and into a town. They were excited and nervous at the same time: they were going to meet a king! Was it possible that the king, or someone here in the palace, was the person who was going to help them get back to Ithaca?

Ithaca island, Ionian sea, Greece.

CHAPTER 15

Help at Last

They were quite embarrassed at the way they looked. No one looks that good after being shipwrecked. So it was with great relief that they were taken into the palace and given a place to clean up.

After they were ready, they were led to an enormous hall. At the front of the hall sat the king, and beside him, the queen.

"Please come forward," said the king.

They were even more relieved when they heard him speak perfect English.

"What are your names?" asked the king.

"I'm Max," said Max. "And these are my friends, Kathy and Brad."

"Welcome Max, Kathy and Brad," said the king. "What is the name of the land of your people?"

"We come from a place called Ithaca," answered Max.

"I have heard of this place," said the king.

"We have sailed for many days and now we have lost our ship," said Max. "Can you help us get back to our home?"

"I will do my best," answered the king. "How and from where did you begin your journey?"

"We were in our town of Ithaca," answered Max. "The three of us were looking at a book, and then, suddenly, everything started spinning around and there was mist and then darkness and then we found ourselves in a boat in the middle of the Mediterranean Sea."

"How fascinating," said the king. "And do you still have this book?"

"Yes," said Max. He had been smart enough to wear his backpack in addition to his life preserver when the storm tossed them overboard.

"Bring it to me," said the king.

Max took it to the king and handed it to him. The king looked at it and then asked Max to show him which map they had been looking at.

"Ah," said the king. "Yes, this is the Mediterranean Sea. And here are our island."

He showed Max and Kathy and Brad exactly where

they were at the moment, and confirmed that they had visited all the islands that they thought they had visited.

"I have an idea," said the king. "Please show me exactly what you were doing just before the spinning and the mist and the darkness started."

"We were sitting on the ground under a tree," said Max.

"Yes," said the king. "Please show me."

So Max sat on the floor of the palace in front of the king. Brad sat on Max's right, and Kathy sat on Max's left just like in Ithaca.

"Yes," said the king. "I see. And the book?"

"I was holding the book and all three of us were looking at it," answered Max.

"Please put the book exactly where it was when you were under the tree," said the king.

Max did as he was asked.

"And was there anything else special happening when the spinning began?" asked the king.

"Yes," answered Max. "We had found the map of the

Mediterranean Sea, and we had found a picture of a monster, and we all pointed at it at the same time."

"Aha," said the king. "And were you all touching the same map at the same time?"

"Yes, I think we were," answered Max.

"I see," said the king. "Now comes the tricky part. Can you find a map in your book that shows your home, the place called Ithaca?"

Max flipped through the pages until he found a map that showed Ithaca.

"Here it is," he said.

"Now I want all three of you to point to the place you call Ithaca," instructed the king. "And now all three of you must touch the place called Ithaca."

They did as they were told and it started happening again. The throne room started to spin around; it started to get dark and misty. They were spinning faster and faster. They all held on tightly to the book.

"It's happening!" yelled Kathy.

When the spinning stopped and the mists began to clear, they were sitting on the grass under the shade tree in Ithaca.

They were silent. They were in shock.

Finally, Max broke the silence.

"Did all of that just happen, or was it a dream?" he asked.

"My clothes are kind of damp," said Kathy.

"I've got some seaweed in my shoe," said Brad.

"Remind me to be careful which books I check out of the library next time," said Max.

THE END